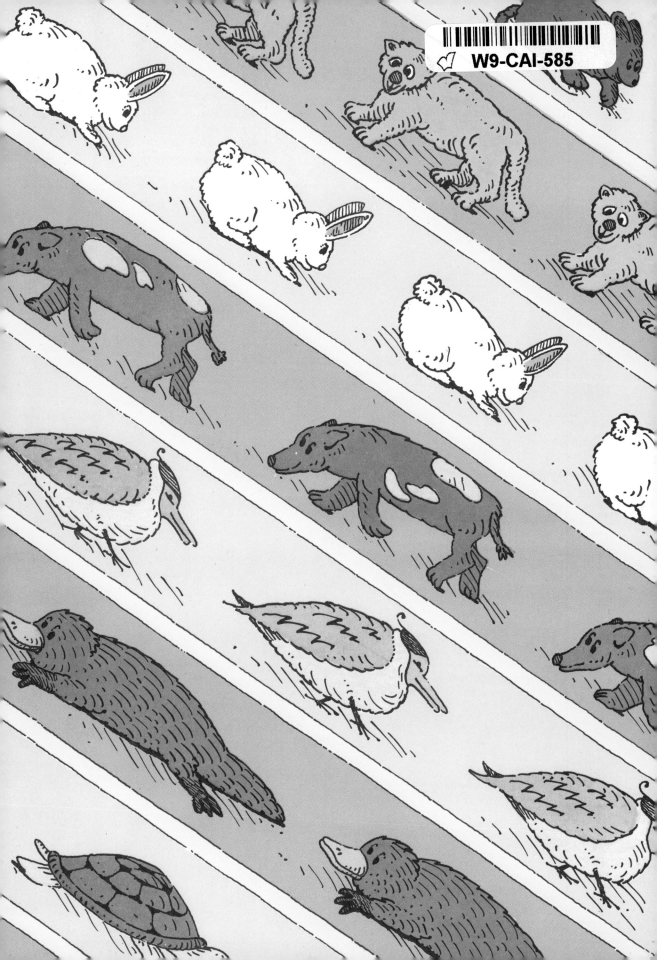

A Story with a Happy Ending

# THE · SPOTTED COW

*Story by Donald Nelsen   Illustrations by Merle Peek*

*Parents' Magazine Press / New York*

Library of Congress Cataloging in Publication Data

Nelsen, Donald.
   The spotted cow.
   SUMMARY: A lady, a cow, a canary, and a princess try
to satisfy their mutual needs without too much sacrifice.
   I. Peek, Merle, illus.     II. Title.
PZ7.N4338Sp          [E]          73-5738
ISBN 0-8193-0694-0   ISBN 0-8193-0695-9  (lib. bdg.)

*To A W N, E E N, B, D, and J*

THERE WAS A LADY who kept a spotted cow. She lived in a tiny house near the palace where the Prince and Princess lived. When asked why she kept the cow, the lady would shrug and say, "Oh, to keep the grass down," but the real reason was that she was very fond of the cow. The cow was about all she owned, except for a few blue dresses and some pots and pans. And, yes, she had a yellow canary, but that was not by choice.

The canary had come upon the cow in the meadow one day, and since then spent all its time fluttering about or riding from pasture to pasture on the cow's back. The cow had grown so used to the canary's singing that now, when the canary flew away for a few hours, or for a whole morning, the cow would become very troubled. She would stop eating and just stand mooing sadly until the canary returned. The lady didn't like the canary very much and thought all its singing and chirping was a little foolish. But she knew it made her cow happy, and she put up with it.

One day the lady was in her apple tree picking apples when the Prince stepped out of the bushes behind her. He had started out from the palace with the Princess, but she had fallen far behind and he was alone. He didn't look like a prince, being rather plump, not young, and very careless in his dress. Today, for instance, the vest of his hunting suit was not buttoned right and one sock had already fallen down.

"You'll have to move from this property," he said, looking up at her.

"Why?" The lady dropped a few apples. She didn't particularly care for her tiny house, but she had never thought of living anywhere else.

"Because I'm planting a rose garden here." The Prince had little to do in life except think of new things to keep from being bored.

"Couldn't you put it somewhere else?"

"Only if I destroy my tennis courts, and that would be ridiculous."

The lady agreed. The Prince had put in tennis courts the year before and they were very pretty, although no one ever used them.

At that moment the Princess came through the bushes. "Don't worry, dear lady," she said grandly as she approached. "We'll find a place for you."

The Princess was younger than her husband and not as plump. Unlike him, she was very concerned about her appearance, and today she wore a gown that was so elaborate it made it difficult for her to walk, which is why she had fallen so far behind.

"Now then," she said, opening a velvet notebook. "How many of

you are there?" The Princess prided herself on doing good deeds, but
selected only those which required no sacrifice.

"How many what?" asked the lady.

"How many in your family?"

"Just me and the spotted cow."

The Princess looked up. "A cow?"

"To keep the grass down," and the lady pointed to the backyard
where the cow was grazing.

The Princess stared for a moment, then snapped her notebook shut. "Disgusting beast!" She turned to the Prince. "We shall find a home for this dear lady, but the cow must go somewhere else."

The lady was about to say that she would not be separated from her cow, when the canary fluttered down from the sky and settled on the cow's back, bursting into trills and warbles.

The Princess clapped her hands together and beamed. "I *love* it."

"Just a wild canary," shrugged the lady, climbing down from the tree.

"I *want* it." She turned to the Prince. "Get me that canary."

The Prince stuttered and stammered and finally said, "But—"

"Oh, you blockhead," cried the Princess, and she grabbed the hat from his head, marched up to the cow and plunked it down over the singing bird. "There!" she said triumphantly. And bundling the hat together at the brim, she marched quickly toward the bushes, in spite of her gown. The Prince followed at her heels.

The lady was too stunned to speak for a moment. Then she called after them. "You can't take the canary!"

"Why not?" asked the Princess, already half-hidden by the bushes. "He's wild. You said so yourself. He's not yours."

The lady said quietly, "You're a mean old thing."

"So are you," answered the Princess, and she and the Prince were gone, leaving the lady and the spotted cow alone on the grass.

Several hours later the cow raised her head and looked around, very puzzled. Then she began to moo softly and give long troubled sighs.

"There, there," the lady comforted, "there must be other canaries." But she didn't remember ever having seen any.

Days passed and the cow grew more unhappy. She stopped eating altogether and spent her time mooing sadly. The lady watched as the cow grew thinner and sadder, and finally, on the fourth day, the lady

put on a clean blue dress and walked up the path to the palace. A foot-man let her in at the front door and took her through halls and cor-ridors and empty rooms.

"This is certainly a big place for just the two of them," said the lady, meaning the Prince and Princess.

The footman made no answer. At last he led her into an empty banquet hall where the Princess sat staring into a cold fireplace.

The lady eyed the beautiful gold cage in which the canary sat, huddled and silent.

"You must give me back the canary," she said.

"Why should I?"

"Because my cow needs him."

"So do I."

"No. You only *want* him. There's a difference. My cow won't eat unless the canary's there. Somehow she can't live without that foolish singing."

"Then you're out of luck." The Princess laughed meanly. "That bird hasn't made a peep since he got here."

"Well, of course not. The canary won't sing without the cow."

"That's ridiculous!" shouted the Princess.

The lady went back home.

The Princess stared into the fireplace for a few moments and then got up and went out on the terrace where the Prince was chatting with a maid. "Build me a barn," she ordered shrilly, as the maid scurried away.

"What for?" asked the surprised Prince.

"For the spotted cow, you blockhead. And hire a stableman to tend her." And she went back to the cold fireplace.

The lady with the spotted cow was in her yard the next morning when a carriage stopped and the Princess leaned out of the window. "I've come to buy the spotted cow."

"Not for sale," said the lady.

"I'll give you a lot of money."

There was no answer.

The Princess squinted up her eyes and shouted, "You're a mean old thing!"

"Maybe," said the lady, "but so are you."

The Princess rolled up the window and ordered the coachman to drive away.

A week passed and the Princess could think of no way to get the cow. Nor could the lady get the canary. The situation seemed entirely hopeless, and finally the lady decided that no good could come of it and that she would just move away. She packed her blue dresses and some pots and pans and led the cow through the bushes and onto the path that would take them past the palace to the nearby town.

"There, there," she said, one arm over the cow's neck. "We'll find you a canary." The cow gave a long whimpering moo.

As they passed the palace, they paused for a moment to admire the beautiful new barn that stood by the Prince's tennis courts. Then they moved on, clip-clop . . . clip-clop, very slowly.

Inside, the Princess still sat staring into the fireplace. She heard the clip-clopping sound, but paid no attention. Then she heard another sound and she leaped to her feet. The canary was singing! It was singing in its cage, as bright and cheerful as could be. She heard, too, the spotted cow bellowing happily, and she ran out of the palace and down to where the lady stood, laughing and hugging the spotted cow. The cow was arching her back happily and dancing a little on clumsy feet.

"Where do you think you're going?" demanded the Princess.

"Away."

"You can't!" the Princess shouted. She stopped, trying to control herself, and her voice was softer as she said, "Leave the cow with me. *Please*. I'll take good care of her."

The lady shook her head and began tugging at the cow, who was nibbling grass now from the side of the road.

"But the canary's singing at last. Can't you hear?" the Princess pleaded. "Don't take the cow away."

The lady said nothing. The cow had begun to move, very slowly, one foot at a time.

"You're a mean old thing," the Princess said weakly, but there was no answer.

The lady and the spotted cow were moving away now. Inside the palace the canary stopped singing. The Princess looked about frantically, fluttering her hands. She gave a long exhausted sigh, seeming to grow smaller in her velvet gown. "All right," she said, in a tiny tired voice. And then she did exactly what she had been trying not to do all along. She did a good deed. "Come live in the palace," she said. "It's too big for the Prince and me. You could have the whole second floor. Just bring the spotted cow."

"That would be fine," said the lady, turning the cow around in the path. She had been thinking of exactly that for several days, but hadn't known how to suggest it.

And that's what finally happened. The lady moved into the second floor of the palace and kept her spotted cow.

The Princess listened to the canary whenever she pleased, and the Prince planted a rose garden that was so beautiful he was never bored again.

The lady with the spotted cow and the Princess never became
friends, quite, and they found very little to say to each other. But they
often sat together on the lawn, watching the cow and listening to the
canary.

Now and then they played tennis.

None of them would have admitted it, perhaps, but they were all much happier.

*Donald Nelsen* held several editing and commercial writing jobs before 1959, when he received a Fulbright grant in painting. He holds a B.F.A. degree from Antioch College and has studied painting in Paris and at the Brooklyn Museum School of Art. Mr. Nelsen grew up in Wisconsin and Indiana and still considers himself a Hoosier, even though for some thirteen years he has lived in Brooklyn. He is the author of *Sam and Emma*, also published by Parents' Magazine Press.

*Merle Peek* was born in Denver, Colorado, and received his B.F.A. from the California College of Arts and Crafts in Oakland. After several years working in New York City—on the staff of *Time* and *New York Magazine*—he now lives in the Catskill Mountains near Woodstock, New York, where he is an enthusiastic organic gardener. During the winter he travels and has been around the world once.